Burn Up

Spike T. Adams

Illustrated by Oliver Harud

W
FRANKLIN WATTS
LONDON•SYDNEY

Chapter 1

"Hand me that spanner, Jay," Dad called.

I was on my way out to school.

"You'll never flog this piece of junk," I told him, handing over the spanner.

"You just watch me," he said. "It's going in the paper today."

I put my bag down. "It'll be finished loads quicker if I help."

Dad stopped and looked at me.

He nodded. "Yeah..."

I grinned at him.

He grinned back. "But you ain't missing school."

Crap. He'd busted me.

I grabbed up my bag and left.

So later I was coming out of one boring lesson.

On my way into another.

Then I heard this voice.

"You're Jay, right?"

It was Kyle from the year above.

He was with his mate Grant.

"Word is you're tasty with the tools."

I couldn't believe they were talking to me.

Let alone knew my name.

"Friends of ours got car trouble," Grant went on. "Wanna help out?"

I shrugged. "Could do..."

I was playing it cool.

But inside I was well pleased.

"Back gate, four o'clock?" Kyle asked.

"I'll be there," I said.

They nodded and began to walk away.

People gave them respect as they passed.

No wonder.

They were sharp. They had friends with cars.

Grant turned and called over his shoulder.
"See ya later then, Jay."

I couldn't stop grinning.

Everyone gets told by these guys.

I get asked.

Chapter 2

Kyle and Grant took me to meet Ian and Mikey.

I'd never seen them around school.

Figured they must have left.

"Well here's the car."

Mikey popped the hood. "Gonna take a look for us then?"

I put my bag down and rolled up my sleeves.

Kept my cool.

Turned out to be an easy fix.

Kinda thing I can do with one hand behind my back.

An hour later.

"It's sorted," I said. "Just go easy on it."

Mikey jabbed my shoulder.

Ian smiled and nodded at Kyle and Grant.

"This could be sweet for our crew," he said.

11

Didn't think it could get any better.

But then Chantelle came by.

Shanice was with her, as usual.

They were in the same class as me.

Chantelle had it all going on.

The guys knew it. She knew it.

Ian went, "Wanna come for a ride later?"

Chantelle went, "I might."

Kyle went, "You can sit on my lap."

She went, "Promises, promises..."

And then she smiled. Even at me.

My heartbeat went turbo.

Shanice pulled Chantelle away.
"Come on," she said.

Acting like we weren't even there.

We watched them go.

Then Ian turned to Mikey.

"What's with your sister?" he asked. "Shooting us evils all the time!"

Mikey shrugged. "Training to be Saint Shanice," he said.

"Either that or she's just frigid."

They all laughed.

For a second I felt bad.

But then I laughed too.

So what? Main thing was, they seemed to like me.

It would be so cool to join their crew.

Chapter 3

Next day in school, Chantelle pulled out a chair.

"Hey, Jay. Wanna sit next to me?"

I shrugged, and then nodded.

Tried to keep it cool.

But she knew I liked her.

And I mean like with a capital 'L'.

I sat down and smiled at her.

She smiled back.

But there was Saint Shanice.

Rolling her eyes. Shaking her head.

Spoiling it.

What was with her?

Chapter 4

A few days later, Kyle and Grant called on me again.

I went with them to the same garage.

Only there was a different car in it.

"Like it?" he asked me.

"What's not to like?" I said.

The car must have cost somebody a bomb.

And no way was it Ian.

"Kind owner left the keys in for us," Ian told me.

The others laughed.

"Stupid wanker — deserved to have it nicked," said Kyle.

Alarm bells were ringing in my head.

"You gonna keep your mouth shut?" Mikey asked me.

What did he think I was gonna do?

Run to the police?

I wanted to be in their crew.

So I nodded. Like it was nothing.

"Cool," Mikey said. He put an arm on my shoulder.

"Thing is, we've driven this baby hard, man."

"Yeah, engine keeps cutting out now," Ian went on. "Will ya sort it for us?"

"OK," I said.

Chantelle wasn't at school the next day.

I was gutted.

But Shanice was there. She kept looking at me.

And then she kissed her teeth at me.

That was it.

"What's your problem?" I asked her.

"You," she said. "You are a total idiot — hanging out with that crew."

She turned away.

I wanted to hit back — say something like, "At least I'm not frigid!"

But the bell went for end of lesson.

So I left it.

Chapter 5

Ian wanted me to look at another car at the weekend.

Only this time he didn't even have the keys.

"What was up with the other one?" I asked.

"Had to dump it – we got seen," Ian told me.

"This one will be more fun," said Mikey, grinning.

"When we get it going again," Ian added.

They all looked at me.

I felt like walking away. This was getting too hot.

Then Chantelle and Shanice came by.

Chantelle looked at the car and then at me.

She smiled.

So I began to fix their botched hotwire job.

In the corner of my eye I saw Shanice walk away.

But Chantelle stayed.

Ian revved the engine. "Nice work, Jay," he said. "You coming?"

He pointed to the front seat, next to him.

Now I really was part of the crew.

I shrugged, and then got in. Playing it cool.

The other guys got in the back.

"I'll ride on your lap Jay," Chantelle said.

I could hardly speak as she pressed her body close to mine.

I put my hands round her waist.

She didn't complain.

Ian put his foot down.

It felt so great, riding around.

Hanging out with my crew. A hot girl on my lap.

This was the life.

Maybe Chantelle would go out with me if I asked.

"Keep a look out for something tasty," Ian called to the guys.

Then Grant said, "Look — over there!"

Across the road was a silver Peugeot.

Ian circled round the block.

"Oh, wow! Get it! Get it!" screamed Chantelle.

Mikey scoped the streets — all clear.

We all watched as he went across.

He took a thin metal bar from inside his jacket.

But it didn't work.

So he hit the window.

A loud ringing started. The car was alarmed.

Mikey ran back to our car.

"Go! Go!" he shouted.

Ian hit the gas hard.

31

We found another car.

No alarm this time.

Mikey popped the lock and hotwired the engine.

The engine growled as Mikey floored the pedal.

"Come on Grant!" he yelled.

Grant got out to join Mikey in the other car.

So Chantelle took his place in the back.

I felt gutted.

She didn't want to sit on my lap. She'd just been waiting for a space.

The two cars roared off.

Chapter 6

We drove to the other side of town.

There was nobody around.

Mikey had got there before us.

Ian pulled up next to him.

"What took you so long?" Mikey shouted.

Chantelle giggled. "He's been driving like an old man."

Ian was well annoyed. He gripped the steering wheel tight.

"Three times round the estate — loser buys the booze," he said.

"Deal," said Mikey.

They touched fists.

My heart thumped. I pulled on my seatbelt.

But we were off before I could clip it in.

Mikey was driving a better car.

But Ian had the moves. And the guts.

He kept his foot on the floor.

Never took it off for a second.

Pushed it to 60 mph. Then 70.

The tyres screamed. The whole car shook
and shuddered.

We drifted round corners like they weren't there.

We all just kept laughing.

Loving every second of it.

It was neck and neck.

And then somebody yelled, "Police!"

I looked round — saw flashes of blue as the sirens started.

The police began to get closer.

Ian's speedo went up to 90.

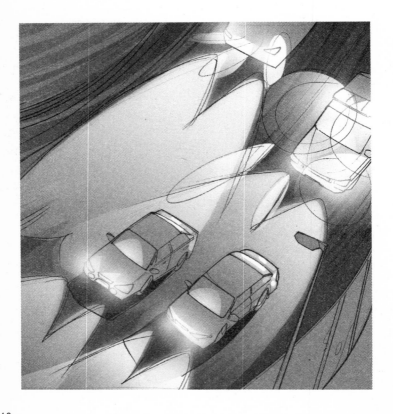

Then the rain came down.

Splashing against the windscreen.

Making it hard to see. Soaking the road.

We slipped and slid along.

Swerved out of control. But Ian held it.

No matter what we did – the police were always there.

We took another corner. A girl stepped out.

"Ian!" I yelled.

Ian turned the wheel hard.

We swerved up onto the pavement and missed the girl by millimeters.

As we sped along I looked back.

The girl was just staring at us, in shock.

She was lucky to be alive.

So was I.

If I got out of this...

me and this whole crew...

we were OVER!

Chapter 7

The cars screeched to a halt in the middle of an estate.

I smashed my knee on the dash.

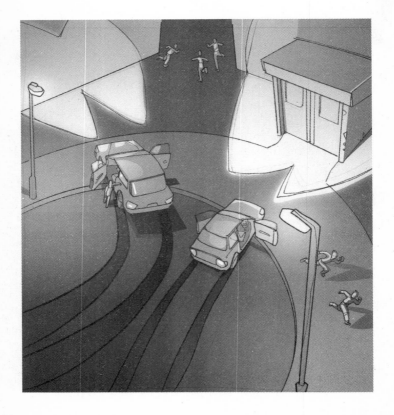

Before I knew it, the crew had scattered.

I just stood there, alone.

I looked around at all the closed doors.

I could hear the sirens getting louder.

I limped to the nearest intercom.

Pressed a button. Pressed them all.

Shouted for help.

Nobody came.

The police cars skidded and stopped.

With nowhere to hide, I got ready to take the rap.

I felt really bad as I wondered what Dad
would say.

But then someone grabbed me.

I looked round.

Saint Shanice!

She said nothing. Just dragged me inside
the block.

Shanice pulled me into a dark cupboard and shut the door.

We were pressed tight together.

I could feel her heart beating — as fast as mine.

Someone let the police in.

We breathed quietly as they asked around.

They knocked at every flat.

It seemed to take hours.

We were boiling.

Then finally they left.

Shanice pushed me out.

I wanted to thank her but she held up her hand.

"Save it!" she snapped.

And she hurried away.

Chapter 8

My bed had never felt so good.

But I got no sleep.

In my head, I could still hear the police sirens.

And the voice of some judge, sending me down.

I could see Dad's sad face as he watched.

And then I remembered Shanice.

She'd saved me. Sorted me out.

She'd felt good, close up.

Really good.

And now my head was filled with her.

I got to school on Monday feeling wasted.

Kyle and Grant were hanging out with Chantelle and Shanice.

Chantelle saw me and giggled. "Enjoy yourself the other night, Jay?" she asked.

Shanice looked away.

That hurt more than Chantelle's teasing.

"What's the matter Jay?" said Kyle.

"Didn't they look after you down at the nick?"

"I didn't end up at the nick," I told him coldly.

"Someone helped me out. And that's more than you did."

"Don't be like that, mate," said Grant. "You just need to run a bit faster."

He, Kyle and Chantelle couldn't stop laughing.

But I didn't laugh.

"So, it's on again tonight," Kyle went on. "Mikey's got some sweet rides lined up."

I shook my head. "Not me."

Chantelle's eyes opened wide.

"What?" Grant asked.

"Count me out," I said.

Kyle and Grant both looked at me.

"You're making a big mistake," Kyle said.

But I didn't flinch.

"I don't think so," I said.

They walked off, still looking at me.

Chantelle watched Kyle and Grant go.

She grabbed Shanice's arm. "Come on Shan," she said.

But Shanice yanked her arm back.

Chantelle frowned like she couldn't believe it.

Right then I knew.

Shanice wasn't a saint.

She was just strong.

Chantelle shrugged. "Suit yourself."

She hurried off to follow Kyle and Grant.

"I owe you one," I said.

Shanice folded her arms. "Well... If you're really grateful you can show me how to strip an engine."

I stared at her. "You serious?"

She laughed. Cutest laugh I'd ever heard.

"I'm not gonna nick cars!" she said. "I just always wanted to be a mechanic."

I took her hand. It was small, but strong.

Good for working with engines.

And it fitted into my hand just right.

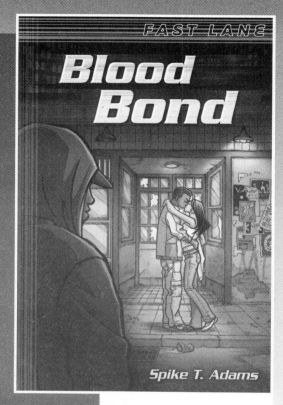

978 0 7496 7712 1

Devon has two older brothers.

One rolls with the Endz Crew. The other is seeing a Viper Crew girl.

The two gangs don't mix.

Then someone pulls a gun...

FAST LANE

Snap Kick

Spike T. Adams

978 0 7496 7715 2

Amir wants to play for the school football team — the Hill Street Hawks.

The Stone Crew have other ideas.

But Amir won't be pushed around...

FAST LANE

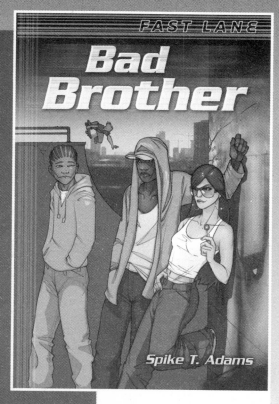

978 0 7496 7713 8

Tyler is vexed.

He's had to give up half of his room, his mum cusses him and the girl he likes plays hard to get.

And all cos of one idiot person — Alex, his stupid step-brother.

Time to get this sorted...

ASKHAM BRYAN
COLLEGE
LEARNING RESOURCES